Tippy
Finds a Home

By Mary Beth Stevens
Illustrated by Susan Spellman

Peter E. Randall Publisher
Portsmouth, NH
2019

ISBN: 978-1-942155-20-1
Library of Congress Control Number: 2018963945
Published by
Peter E. Randall Publisher
Box 4726
Portsmouth, NH 03802
www.perpublisher.com

Book design by Tim Holtz

Dedication

While many parts of our country are overrun with
homeless dogs, other parts of the country simply don't
have enough adoptable dogs to meet local needs.
Dogs are now being transported hundreds—even
thousands—of miles by cars, trucks, vans, tractor trailers,
and even airplanes to be placed with loving families.
This book is dedicated to the dogs and to the many, many
volunteers along the way who make it possible for them
to find their loving, forever homes.

This is a true story.

"My word," thought Tippy-the-Terrier. "Where in the world AM I?"

He knew he was supposed to be finding his forever home, but he had NEVER imagined anything like THIS! He was in a cage in the back of a big truck filled with other dogs in cages. Some were sleeping, some were pacing, some were howling, and some were yowling, but Tippy just sat quietly.

"Where am I going?" he wondered. "Just where IS this forever home I am supposed to find?"

After traveling for hours and hours, sometimes napping but sometimes just worrying, Tippy found himself in a busy building filled with people and dogs.

"What a hubbub!" he thought to himself, but time passed, and after a good meal and a good night's sleep, Tippy woke up feeling refreshed and ready to go.

"Maybe THIS is the day," he thought. "The day I find my forever family!"

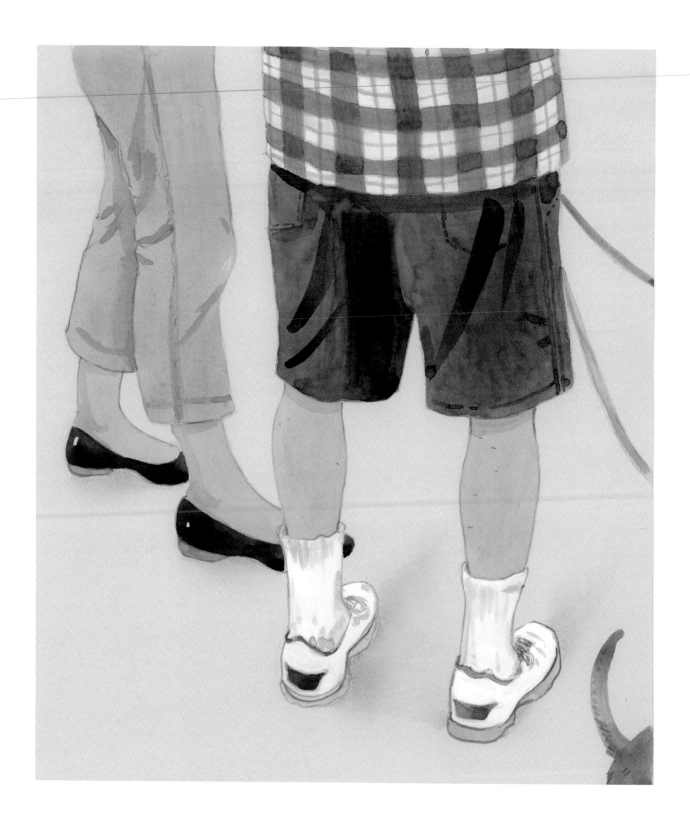

Before long, a Nice Woman and Nice Man came into the room. They led Tippy to their car and introduced him to a little brown dog named Suzie.

"Tippy," the Nice Woman said, "We're going to be your foster family. You'll stay with us while you search for your forever home."

"Oh dear," thought Tippy. "A foster family? I thought I was supposed to find a FOREVER family!"

But Tippy was a polite little dog, so he looked at Suzie and said, "Hello, Suzie," all the while thinking to himself, "Look at her ears! They're huge! Her ears make me laugh!"

But then he saw her collar…

"Oh my!" he exclaimed to himself. "What a beautiful collar! It's purple! And her name is stitched on it with pink thread! I've never seen anything quite so fine!"

Tippy's foster family brought him to their house in the woods where he met Toby-the-Cat. "Oh dear," thought Tippy. "A cat. I know ALL about cats! They're kind of snooty and particular, and they know NOTHING about how to play. I'll just avoid him and hope that my forever family doesn't have any cats!"

The Nice Woman and Nice Man showed Tippy all around their house in the woods.

He found toys to play with,

comfy beds to sleep in,

and a big yard—perfect for playing fetch and chase.

But Tippy was a handful—he wasn't a bad dog, but he was a BUSY dog. He ran through the house, ate the garbage, chewed the furniture, tore up the toys, stepped on Toby-the-Cat, and wriggled under the fence three times in one day. He snored when he slept, and he bounced when he was awake. There was simply no slowing him down.

The Nice Woman and Nice Man set to work trying to teach Tippy manners. "Sit! Sit," they repeated. "Come!" "Stay!"

"That doesn't sound like much fun—all of that sitting and coming and staying," thought Tippy. "I'd much rather romp and tear around the house." And so he did.

And as Tippy and Suzie began to get to know each other,
it was a little rocky at first…

"Grrr…," said Tippy. "That's MY toy! I saw it first!"

"No, it isn't," said Suzie. "It's MY toy, I was here before you!"

"Grrr…," said Suzie, the first time Tippy tried to jump up into the Nice
Man's lap for a nap. "That's MY Papa, not yours! You get out of here!"

"Sheesh," said Tippy. "THAT's not very nice!" But he jumped down and curled up in a corner of the room. "She hears everything with those big ears of hers," he grumbled to himself.

"Tippy, Suzie, please," said the Nice Woman. "You're both wrong. Here at the house in the woods we have plenty of toys and plenty of laps. In fact, we have plenty of love—there is more than enough love for everyone. We'll have no more of this foolishness between the two of you."

So Tippy and Suzie began the process of learning to share. They shared toys and laps, yummy treats and car rides, walks in the big woods, and naps in front of the fireplace.

Out in the world, Tippy made friends everywhere he went. "Hi!" he said. "I'm Tippy! Who are you?" And everyone would smile.

And then one day when the Nice Woman asked Tippy and Suzie to sit, Tippy, well…. TIPPY … JUST … SAT! And no one was more surprised than he was. "Hey!" said Tippy. "Look at me! I can do this! I can DO this!" And a proud little smile came over his terrier face.

But all the while he thought about his forever home. "Where are they, this forever family of mine?" he wondered. "What will they be like, and how will I find them? How will THEY find ME here in this house in the woods?"

One day a volunteer from the animal rescue organization called the Nice Woman. "We're trying to find the perfect family for Tippy, and since you know him better than anyone, we hope you can help us. Can you describe his perfect forever home? Where would he be happiest?"

So, the Nice Woman sat down with a pencil and started to think…

"Well," she said to herself, "Tippy needs lots of love, but he also needs some rules. He needs someone who will take him places and train him to be a good dog. He'd love a doggy brother or sister, and he loves playing and car rides and running in the woods…."

"Oh dear," she thought to herself….and she went to talk to the Nice Man.

"When I sat down to write a description of the perfect home for Tippy," she said, "it ended up sounding exactly like OUR home."

"Oh no," said the Nice Man. "He's a rascal."

"A scamp," she added. "And a terror…He's a handful!"

They went on and on until the Nice Man finally sputtered, "That little dog is a…a…a, well…he's a RAPSCALLION!"

"You're right," said the Nice Woman. "Tippy is all of those things. He IS a rascal and a scamp and a terror and even a rapscallion. But at this point, it feels like he's OUR rapscallion. He needs us, but I think WE need HIM, too. Things have gotten entirely too quiet and calm around here. Tippy shakes things up, but in a good way.

And he's come so far! Just look how happy he makes Suzie! She can be shy, but Tippy leads the way and shows her how to make new friends."

They sat quietly for a few minutes, and then they made their decision.

That night at bedtime, the Nice Woman and Nice Man began to tuck all the animals into their beds.

"Goodnight, Toby-the-Cat," they said. "Sweet dreams."

"Goodnight, Suzie," they said. "Sweet dreams."

"Tippy," they said. "This is for you." And they handed Tippy a small, carefully-wrapped package.

Tippy tore it open, and there—THERE!—was a beautiful red collar with his name stitched in blue thread.

"For me?" said Tippy. "For me? Really?"

"Yes, really," they said. "Your search is over. You've found your forever home, and it is right here with all of us. We will keep you and take good, good care of you. You and Suzie can run and play and snuggle forever."

Tippy looked up at both of them and his brown eyes sparkled. "I get to stay here in the house in the woods with you and Suzie and Toby-the-Cat? That means my search is over! I've found my forever home, and it is right here with all of YOU! This is the best news ever!" And a happy tear trickled down the side of his little terrier nose.

"That's right, Tippy. Welcome to the family. From now on WE will be your Mama and Papa, just like we are to Suzie and Toby-the-Cat."

"Oh, GOOD!" said Tippy, as he buried his head in his snuggly doggy bed and looked forward to happy doggy dreams.

"Oh, GOOD!" said Suzie, as she did the same, dreaming of days and days of chasing Tippy through the woods and across the fields.

"Oh, DEAR!" said Toby-the-Cat. "I guess he isn't leaving after all..."

And he flicked his tail and sauntered out of the room.